Amy HODGEPODGE
LOST AND FOUND

BY KIM WAYANS & KEVIN KNOTTS
ILLUSTRATED BY SOO JEONG

Grosset & Dunlap

OCT 08

CH

For Elvira, Howell, Billie, and Ivan.
And for Sylvia—the best teacher ever.

GROSSET & DUNLAP
Published by the Penguin Group
Penguin Group (USA) Inc., 375 Hudson Street, New York, New York 10014, USA
Penguin Group (Canada), 90 Eglinton Avenue East, Suite 700, Toronto, Ontario
M4P 2Y3, Canada (a division of Pearson Penguin Canada Inc.)
Penguin Books Ltd., 80 Strand, London WC2R 0RL, England
Penguin Group Ireland, 25 St. Stephen's Green, Dublin 2, Ireland
(a division of Penguin Books Ltd.)
Penguin Group (Australia), 250 Camberwell Road, Camberwell, Victoria 3124, Australia
(a division of Pearson Australia Group Pty. Ltd.)
Penguin Books India Pvt. Ltd., 11 Community Centre, Panchsheel Park,
New Delhi—110 017, India
Penguin Group (NZ), 67 Apollo Drive, Rosedale, North Shore 0632, New Zealand
(a division of Pearson New Zealand Ltd.)
Penguin Books (South Africa) (Pty.) Ltd., 24 Sturdee Avenue,
Rosebank, Johannesburg 2196, South Africa

Penguin Books Ltd., Registered Offices:
80 Strand, London WC2R 0RL, England

Copyright © 2008 Gimme Dap Productions, LLC.
Published by Grosset & Dunlap, a division of Penguin Young Readers Group,
345 Hudson Street, New York, New York 10014. GROSSET & DUNLAP is a trademark of
Penguin Group (USA) Inc. Printed in the U.S.A.

Library of Congress Cataloging-in-Publication Data is available.

ISBN 978-0-448-44897-8   10 9 8 7 6 5 4 3 2 1

Chapter 1

"I *love* assemblies!" I told my friends Lola, Pia, and Rusty as we walked down the hall toward the Emerson Charter School auditorium. Our teacher, Mrs. Clark, had just announced that we were having an assembly instead of English. "But I wonder what this one's about."

Lola shrugged. "Maybe someone's coming to speak to us."

"You mean like that artist who came to talk last month?" Pia said. "That would be cool."

"I don't think that's it," Rusty said with a grin. "They probably want to tell us the building is condemned and they have to cancel school for the rest of the year!"

Everyone laughed, including me. But I also shuddered a little. My friends might be happy if school was canceled. But not me! I had only been at Emerson for a short while. Before that I had been homeschooled my whole life. When my dad got a new job and we moved to Dyver City, I told my family that I wanted to try regular school. They weren't sure it was a good idea at first, but they agreed to let me try. At first, school had been hard and kind of scary. Then I'd met a group of really amazing friends. After that I loved school!

When we reached the auditorium, we saw Lola's twin brother, Cole, and our other friends Jesse and Maya. They're in the other class of the fourth grade—Mrs. Musgrove's class. We took seats next to them in the second row.

"Hi, you guys," Jesse greeted us. "This assembly is probably going to be boring. I bet it's about fire drills or something like that."

"Rusty thinks they're going to cancel school forever," Pia said with a giggle.

I was looking around the auditorium. Only the first few rows were filled.

"They're definitely not going to cancel

school," I said. "Otherwise this assembly would be for everyone. It looks like it's just us fourth-graders."

Just then Principal Brewster walked onto the stage. "Good morning, students," he said. He stuck both hands behind his suspenders and rocked back on his heels. That made his large, round stomach look even larger and rounder. "I've brought you all here for an important announcement. It's one I think you're going to like."

"Whoo-hoo! Pizza for lunch all week!" Rusty called out.

Most of the kids started to laugh and cheer. Principal Brewster frowned and peered down at us. Both he and Mrs. Musgrove looked around, trying to figure out exactly who had called out. I was a little worried. I didn't want Rusty to get in trouble. I also didn't want anything to get in the way of me hearing this important announcement.

Principal Brewster cleared his throat. "No,

nothing like that," he said. "This is even better.
Two weeks from now, the entire fourth grade
will be going on a fall wilderness overnight trip.
You'll be spending two nights and two-and-a-
half days at a camp in the woods upstate."

"Wow, cool!" I burst out without thinking.
Then I clapped one hand over my mouth. Luckily,
nobody noticed. That's because everyone else
was talking, too. This was big news!

"I love camping!" Jesse said as we all headed
back to our classrooms after the assembly. "My

family has gone camping at the beach, like, five times."

"And I went to sleepaway camp last summer! It was the best!" Pia exclaimed. "I even found a way to make my plain camp T-shirt look cute!"

"Really? You've all been camping before?" I asked. My friends nodded, and suddenly I started to feel nervous. "Um, I've never been camping," I admitted. "Actually, I've never spent the night away from my family."

"Are you serious?" Cole stared at me. His brown eyes were wide with surprise.

Maya patted me on the arm. "Don't worry, Amy," she said. "We'll show you what to do."

"Yeah," Lola said. "This trip is going to be 'amazing!"

She grinned at me and held up her hand. I gave her a high five and smiled back. What was I worried about? Lola was right. So what if I hadn't gone camping before? My friends would help me, just like they'd helped me learn about regular school. And we would all have a blast!

❁ ❁ ❁

"Hi, everyone!" I yelled as I burst through the front door that afternoon. "Guess what?"

My parents and grandparents hurried in from different directions. My mom's parents—the Kims—live with us. It's great having them around all the time.

My dog, Giggles, ran in, too. He hopped on his hind legs and barked. He can always tell when I'm excited or happy about something. It makes him happy and excited, too.

"It's the best news! I can't believe it! Principal

Brewster!" I exclaimed. I was so excited that my words came out all jumbled, so I just waved the packet that our teachers had handed out after the assembly. It contained a permission slip and information about the trip.

My dad took it out of my hand and looked through it. "Hmm, it looks like Amy's entire grade is invited on an overnight camping trip," he told my mom and grandparents.

"Isn't that awesome?" I cried. "I can't wait to sleep in a tent and cook over a campfire! It's going to be so much fun!"

I grabbed Giggles and gave him a hug. He licked my face. I got a whiff of his smelly breath. One of these days I'm going to have to invent some doggy mouthwash.

My grandmother clapped her hands. "It sounds like a wonderful adventure, Little Mitsukai!" she said. That's her nickname for me. She's from Japan, and Little Mitsukai is Japanese for "Little Angel."

My grandfather nodded. "Wonderful, Amy," he agreed.

He doesn't have a Japanese nickname for me. That's because he's Korean and doesn't speak Japanese. That means I'm half Asian (one-quarter Korean and one-quarter Japanese). And since my dad is half African-American and half Caucasian, that makes me one-quarter of each! Some of my friends are mixed race, too, but since I'm a mix of *four* different races, Lola gave me the nickname Amy Hodgepodge.

My parents didn't say anything for a moment. I looked over at them just in time to see them trade a worried look.

"What's wrong?" I asked.

My father sighed and rubbed his chin. "I'm just not sure about this, Amy," he said. "After all, this trip involves two nights away from home . . ."

"That's right," Mom cut in. "And you've never spent the night apart from us before. Let alone gone camping."

My heart sank. "But Mom!" I began.

"I'm sorry, Amy," she said, shaking her head. "I'm just not sure this trip is a good idea."

Chapter 2

I couldn't believe it. I had never thought that my parents might not let me go. This was horrible! I had to change their minds.

"I can't miss this trip!" I blurted out. "All my friends are going, and it's going to be so much fun. Just look at the information. Please?"

Mom looked uncertain, but she took the packet from my dad and she flipped through it. I bit my lip, trying to think of more ways to convince them.

"Oh!" Mom said after a moment. She pulled out a sheet of paper. "Look at this. The school is asking for parent volunteers to come along as chaperones."

My dad's face lit up. "Sounds like the perfect solution," he said to my mother. "You could go along on the trip with Amy."

"Perhaps your grandmother and I should

go along, too," said my grandfather. "Oh my, I haven't been camping since I was a boy."

Yikes. My heart sank. I loved my family, but I definitely didn't want them all coming along on the overnight. How uncool would that be!

"Um, that sounds like fun," I said slowly. "But don't you think I should go on my own? You know—the first time. Otherwise it won't be that different from being at home."

My father chuckled. "Uh-oh. Sounds like someone doesn't want the old folks along embarrassing her in front of all her new school friends."

I felt my cheeks flush. It was terrible, but that really was how I felt.

"It's all right, Little Mitsukai," my grandmother assured me, her eyes twinkling. "We were all young once and wanted time away from our families."

"Long, long ago!" my grandfather agreed.

I took a deep breath. "Mom?" I said, looking at her.

She sighed and glanced down at the packet

again. "I don't know, Amy," she said. "I understand
that you want to have fun with your new friends.
But I'm worried that this could be a little more
than you're ready to handle."

"You were worried about me going to school,
too, remember?" I said. "And look how well that's
working out. Besides, there will be plenty of
adults *and* all my friends will be there. They're
all really experienced campers, so they can help
me if I need it. And Mr. Brewster said there will
be tons of educational lectures on nature and

stuff like that, and also plenty of exercise and fresh air . . ."

My father held up one hand, smiling. "All right, Amy," he said. "You make some good points. Now why don't you take Giggles for a walk while we discuss it?"

Suddenly my throat felt tight, so I just nodded. I'd done all the convincing I could do. Now it was up to them.

Grabbing Giggles's leash, I clipped it to his collar. He knew what that meant. He loves walks! He dragged me to the door, his short tail wagging nonstop.

Usually I like walking Giggles. I always see something new and interesting in the neighborhood. It was autumn, and the leaves were turning pretty new colors every day.

But this time I barely saw any of that. I let Giggles lead the way and just wandered along behind him. I couldn't stop thinking about what was happening back at the house.

What would my parents decide? Giggles

stopped to sniff at some fallen leaves, and I
closed my eyes and tried to imagine what it
would be like if Mom and Dad said no. Principal
Brewster had explained that anyone who didn't
go on the overnight would sit in on the fifth-
graders' classes during those two days. I pictured
myself sitting all by myself at lunch while a
bunch of fifth-graders stared at me and thought
I was a big loser.

"No," I said out loud. I opened my eyes and

shook my head. My grandmother always told me to think positively. That meant she wanted me to imagine the best possible thing instead of the worst. I decided to try it.

Giggles gave a tug on the leash. I followed him over to a patch of dirt. While he rolled around in it, I closed my eyes again. This time I imagined what it would be like if I *did* get to go on the overnight. I pictured myself thanking Mom and Dad and giving them big hugs. Then I imagined arriving at camp with my friends. We would set up our tent, then go exploring, and later we would sit around the campfire and tell stories. I would probably have such a great time I'd never want to sleep inside again!

By the time I finished imagining all that, I was smiling. That image was a lot nicer than the first one!

I turned and hurried back toward the house with Giggles. When I let myself in, I glanced at my grandmother right away. She smiled and winked at me. My heart jumped. Could it be . . . ?

"Well, Amy," Mom said with a sigh. "You convinced us. I suppose we can give this overnight thing a try."

Dad nodded. "We'll sign the permission slip." He smiled, then added, "And don't worry, none of us will be coming along."

I gasped. "Oh my gosh! Thank you so much!"

I thanked them about fifty more times, and gave them big hugs.

Then Mom hurried off to check on dinner and Dad got a phone call. My grandfather wandered toward his room. That left me with my grandmother and Giggles.

Suddenly I started to feel nervous again. "What is it, Little Mitsukai?" my grandmother asked. "You look troubled all of a sudden."

"I guess I'm just a teensy bit worried, Obaasan," I said, biting my lip. *Obaasan* means grandmother in Japanese. "What if Mom and Dad are right? What if I'm not ready?"

She smiled. "You are stronger than you think, Little Mitsukai," she said. "You proved that to us by doing so well at your new school."

I felt kind of proud when she said that. Starting school had been hard—probably much harder than camping would be. My worry faded away, and I felt excited again. "You're right, Obaasan. Thanks," I said, reaching down to ruffle Giggles's fur. "This trip is going to be awesome!"

Chapter 3

The weekend before the overnight, Dad took me shopping at the outdoor store at the mall. The information packet for the trip included a list of everything I was supposed to bring. Almost all of it was stuff I already had, like casual clothes, a raincoat, a flashlight, and a pillow. But I needed a new pair of cargo pants, and I had just outgrown my only pair of hiking shoes. Dad seemed to think I needed a few other things that weren't on the list, too.

Our shopping basket already held a hand-crank lantern, a plastic whistle, a pouch of freeze-dried ice cream, a roll of duct tape, a big bottle of hand sanitizer, and a pair of battery-powered heated socks. I didn't think I would need any of that stuff. But I didn't really mind. I was just glad I was allowed to go on the overnight!

"What about this, too?" my dad said, holding up a small object. It looked sort of like a wristwatch, except it didn't have a strap. Dad said that it was a compass. Instead of telling the time, it told you what direction you were going—north, south, east, or west.

"Sounds good," I said. "Thanks, Dad."

On the way home in the car, I took my new compass out of the bag. It was actually pretty cool.

Dad glanced over. "Which direction are we going now?" he asked.

"East," I said, looking at the direction of the needle on the compass.

"Good job," he said. "Just promise me you'll keep that compass in your pocket while you're on that trip, and your mother and I won't have to worry so much."

❀ ❀ ❀

"Sure you don't want me to wait with you until the bus leaves?" Dad asked as he pulled the car into the school parking lot.

I yawned. It was the morning of the trip. The very, *very* early morning. The bus to the campsite was leaving an hour before the normal start of the school day, so we had to get rides to school instead of taking our usual buses.

"It's okay," I said sleepily. "It looks like everyone else is here already. We'll probably leave really soon."

Dad parked near the bus. Then he helped

me get my duffel bag out of the trunk. Fitting everything in there had been tough! I had to pack my regular stuff, plus all the extra camping gear Dad got me. I'd also added a few extras of my own, like my favorite slippers and a framed photo of Giggles so I wouldn't miss him too much. After all, I'd never been away from him overnight, either. At least I didn't have to worry about fitting my compass in the bag. It was in my pocket, just as I'd promised Dad.

"Have a good time, Amy." Dad gave me a hug. "And be sure to call us if you need us."

"Bye, Dad," I said, hugging him back. There was no way I was going to need to call, but I didn't say that. "See you in two-and-a-half days."

Then I dragged my bag over to the bus. Getting it up the steps wasn't easy. My bag was heavy!

Rory, the class bully, leaned over the front seat to stare at me. "Yo, new girl," he said. "This trip is two nights, not two months!"

Rory had been really mean to me on my first

day of school. He stuck a note that said "dumb girl" on my back.

"I just want to make sure that I brought everything I might need," I told him.

I kind of wished that Rory would help me pull my bag up the steps. But he just sat there and watched while I struggled. Luckily Rusty saw me and came over to help.

"Whoa, what did you pack in here, your brick collection? Your bag is so heavy it's going to make the bus pop a wheelie!" he joked.

I giggled. Rusty was always making funny jokes like that. With one last yank, we got the duffel bag up into the aisle and Rusty went back to his seat. Then it was easier to drag along behind me all the way to the back of the bus where the other bags were piled.

My friends were all on the bus already. Jesse, Pia, and Maya were all squeezed into one seat, and Cole and Rusty were right across the aisle. Lola had saved me a seat next to her in front of the boys.

Jennifer Higgins was sitting by herself in the seat across from us. She wrinkled her nose and stared at my camping outfit.

"Good thing we'll be in the woods, so nobody will see those geeky clothes," she said in a mean voice.

For some reason Jennifer doesn't like me. Actually, she doesn't really like anybody except her two best friends, Liza and Gracie. They were sitting in the seat right ahead of her. They laughed and nudged each other.

Pia rolled her eyes. "Don't listen to her, Amy," she said. "Your new pants are adorable. And those hiking shoes are totally perfect. Um, but you probably won't need that lumberjack hat."

"Oh. Okay, if you say so." I took off the hat and stuck it in my bag. Pia knows everything there is to know about fashion. I trusted her opinions about clothes a lot more than Jennifer's.

"All right, people!" Mrs. Clark leaped up the steps. She always has a lot of energy. She was dressed in a totally cool outfit—camouflage cargo pants, hiking boots, and a tie-dyed sweatshirt. Usually she wears regular teacher-type clothes. "I'm going to take roll, and then we can get rolling!" Mrs. Clark was always saying wacky things like that.

We all cheered. Mrs. Clark started calling our names and checking them off on her clipboard. When she was almost finished, several other adults climbed up the steps. One was the other fourth-grade teacher, Mrs. Musgrove.

"Whoa!" Rusty whispered from behind me. "Check out Mrs. M.'s camping outfit!"

I covered my mouth to keep from giggling.

Mrs. Musgrove usually wears long, black dresses and tons of necklaces and scarves. But today she had on wide green shorts with suspenders, wool kneesocks, a poufy white blouse, and a green hat. She looked like a character from one of my favorite movies, *The Sound of Music*.

Meanwhile one of the other adults came down the aisle toward us. She had blond hair and was wearing bright red lipstick. An expensive-looking purse was slung over her shoulder.

"There you are, Jennifer, darling," the woman said. "Thanks for saving me a seat." She sat down beside Jennifer, crossed her legs, opened her purse, and pulled out a compact.

Jennifer's face turned red. "I *didn't*, Mom," she mumbled. "I think you're supposed to sit with the other grown-ups."

"That's nice, dear," her mom said. She dabbed at her face with a powder puff. It didn't seem like she was even listening to Jennifer.

My eyes widened, and I looked over at Lola.

"Looks like Jennifer's mom is one of the chaperones," she whispered with a grin. "How embarrassing!"

Soon Mrs. Clark finished calling roll. "Okay, everyone's here except Stanley Hermann," she said. "I'd better try to call his—"

"Wait! I'm here, don't leave without me!" a breathless voice called from right outside the bus. It was Stanley, a skinny boy with dark hair in the other fourth-grade class. A second later, he rushed up the steps. He almost tripped on the top step, but he caught himself by grabbing one of the seats. Rory laughed.

"Smooth move, nerd," Rory said. "Hey,

Stanley, didn't anyone tell you that you're not supposed to wear your school shoes camping?"

Stanley looked down at his feet. He was wearing lace-up leather shoes. Everyone else had on either sneakers or hiking shoes.

"That's enough, Rory," Mrs. Clark said with a frown. "Take a seat, Stanley. It's time to leave."

Soon the bus was rolling along the highway out of town. It was a pretty long ride to the camp. But my friends and I had fun on the way. Pia taught us a bunch of songs she'd learned at summer camp. A lot of the kids on the bus seemed to know the songs, but they were all new to me.

In between songs, I looked out the windows. The scenery outside kept looking more and more like the country. After a while there was nothing but deep woods on both sides of the road. And a little while after that, I spotted a big wooden sign. It said WELCOME TO CAMP FALLING LEAF.

"Hey, guys," I cried. "Look! We're here!"

Chapter 4

The bus stopped in front of a giant log cabin. Camp Falling Leaf was a good name for the camp. There were tons of colorful autumn leaves drifting all over the place. The camp counselors were waiting for us on the gravel driveway. There were six of them. They all looked about the same age as my cousins who were in college.

"Welcome, Emerson students!" one of them called out as we got off the bus and shuffled through the leaves on the driveway. He was tall and skinny with bright red hair. "I'm Counselor Carl."

The others introduced themselves, too. All their names started with C. Besides Carl, there was Cleo, Cookie, Cooper, Coco, and Chill. They all seemed really nice and friendly.

"Are those your real names?" Jennifer's friend Liza called out. "They're kind of weird."

"Liza!" Mrs. Clark said with a frown. "That's not a very polite thing to say."

"Sorry," Liza said. But she didn't sound that sorry.

The counselors just laughed. "Maybe they're our real names, or maybe they're not," Counselor Carl said with a grin. "That's our little secret."

"I bet they're not their real names," I whispered to Pia.

"The counselors will take over from here," Mrs. Clark announced. "The rest of the chaperones and I will see you a little later." She waved, then turned and walked into the log building with Mrs. Musgrove and the parent volunteers.

"Okay, you heard her! Girls, grab your gear and come with me," Counselor Cleo called out in a peppy voice. She had big brown eyes and a short blond ponytail. "I'll show you to your cabins. Boys, you go with Counselor Cooper."

"See you later," Lola said to Cole and Rusty.

I grabbed my duffel bag. "Isn't this place cool?" I exclaimed. "I can't wait to see our tent!"

"Me too," Pia agreed. "Let's go!"

We followed Cleo and the other girls along a path through the woods. Our feet crunched on the fallen leaves. My bag was still heavy, but I hardly noticed. There was so much to see! On

the way, Counselor Cleo told us each tent had three bunk beds and that we were allowed to divide ourselves however we wanted, as long as no one was left by themselves.

"Perfect!" I said to Jesse, who was walking beside me.

"Huh?" Jesse blinked and stared at me. "What did you say?"

"I said it's perfect that the tents have three bunks," I explained. "It means the five of us can stay together."

"Oh." Jesse didn't say anything else. Instead she turned to stare at a bird fluttering around in the trees beside the path.

I shrugged. I guessed Jesse was a little distracted by all the excitement.

The girls' tents were in a clearing on the shore of a lake. By the time we got there, Jennifer and her friends were already disappearing into the tent closest to the water. Meanwhile Lola raced ahead toward one at the edge of the trees.

"This one's ours!" she cried. "It's supercute!"

"Um . . . well, it's definitely shabby chic!"
said Pia as she pushed open the tent flap. "I call
the bottom bunk on that side!" She hurried over
and set her pink suitcase on her bed.

The inside of the tent was plain but nice.
There was a wooden floor and a set of bunk
beds along each side and one single bed in the
middle. There were also five wooden cubbies for
our things. It was sunny outside, but the thick
canvas walls and roof of the tent made it dim
and shadowy inside.

"Which bed do you want, Amy?" Maya asked
as she dropped her bags inside the doorway.

"I don't care," I said. "You guys can pick first.
I'm just so excited to be here. Camping is fun
already!"

Pia wrinkled her nose. "It's kind of musty in
here. Let's open the window flaps."

There were big windows on each wall. But
these windows didn't have glass. They were just
flaps of canvas tied at the bottom with string.
There were metal rings at the top, and Pia

quickly rolled up the canvas and tied the rolls to the rings. With the flap out of the way, you could see outside through some mesh fabric. I guess that was to keep the bugs out.

"I'll do this one," I offered.

I easily rolled up the window flap. But the first time I tied it to the rings, it fell down right away. I tried tying it tighter.

"Be careful, Amy," Lola said. "You're pulling the mesh part loose."

"Oops," I said. She was right. My extra-tight knot had stretched the fabric too much. A fly flew in and buzzed around the tent.

"Ick!" Jesse shrieked, jumping up and down and waving her hands to keep the fly away from her. "I hate bugs!"

I gulped, feeling even worse. The fly buzzed past Lola, and she shooed it out the tent door.

"Here, let me show you, Amy." Pia came over and tried to untie the flap. Then she frowned. "Uh-oh, it's all tangled."

"Sorry," I said. Then I backed away and sat

down on the bed next to Maya.

"Never mind," said Maya as she put her arm around my shoulders. "Pia will get it fixed. She's a whiz with anything that's fabric."

Pia's fingers were already loosening my knot. "Yeah, it's okay," she called over her shoulder. "I think I've got it."

I smiled weakly. Maybe camping was a little more complicated than I'd thought. Still, I figured I couldn't be perfect at everything on the very first try.

"Um, I need to use the bathroom," I said as I looked around the tent. I didn't see any doors or anything so I asked, "Where is it?"

Lola giggled. "Bathroom?" she said. "Don't you mean the latrine?"

"What's a latrine?" I asked.

I found out a minute later. It turned out a latrine was like an outdoor toilet, except there was no plumbing. It was just a little shed that contained a deep, stinky hole with a toilet seat built over it. Totally gross!

Still, my friends seemed to think that was

a normal part of camping. So I just held my breath and got out of there as quickly as I could. When I came out, Jennifer was waiting.

"Ew," she said as she looked past me into the latrine. "It stinks."

She made it sound like it was my fault, even though it was already stinky when I got there. She rushed in and slammed the wooden door.

I shrugged and headed back toward my tent. I was really glad I didn't have to share a tent with Jennifer!

When I got inside, Pia was dusting the floor with a broom she'd found behind the door. Maya and Lola were unpacking their stuff into the cubbies. Jesse was lying on her bunk with her eyes closed.

I dragged my duffel to the leftover bed, which was the one over Pia's. A ladder at the end made it easy to climb up there. It was just like climbing into Lola's tree house. Once I flopped on the bed I saw that there was a wide wooden ledge between the edge of the mattress and the wall. I got the picture of Giggles out of my bag and set it on the ledge.

Before I could finish unpacking, we all heard an announcement on the loudspeaker. It told everyone to meet at Campfire Clearing.

"Campfire Clearing?" Jesse said, opening her eyes and sitting up. "Where's that?"

Lola hopped to her feet. "I don't know, but let's find out," she said. "Come on, guys!"

Finding Campfire Clearing turned out to be easy. Counselor Cleo was waiting for us by the path. She led us to a big, open area halfway between our tents and the boys' tents. Our teachers and the chaperones were waiting for us there, along with the boys and the rest of the counselors. There was a charred pit in the middle that was surrounded by stones. Around the fire pit were logs for us to sit on. Cleo said that was where we would have nightly campfires.

"Wow, campfires!" I said. "That sounds really fun." It reminded me of my daydreams about camping.

We spotted Cole and Rusty sitting on one of the logs and sat down with them.

"How's your tent?" Maya asked them.

"Pretty cool," Cole said. "We're bunking with Stanley and Danny."

Before we could talk any more, Mrs. Clark called for attention. "Counselor Carl is going to explain how the next couple of days are going to work," she said. "Listen up, please."

Carl stood up. "We're going to divide you up into three color-coded teams," he said. "We'll have the Yellow Team, the Green Team, and the Orange Team."

"Let's all be on the same team," I whispered to Lola.

She nodded. "Definitely! I want to be Orange."

"You'll separate into teams for most of the activities, but the whole group will come together for meals, evening campfires, and the big nature walk on your last morning here," Carl went on. "The teams have already been chosen at random. First, on the Yellow Team . . ."

He listed off the names of the people on the Yellow Team. I was one of them. Rory, Evelyn, Danny, Jennifer, Yasmin, and a few others were, too. But there were several very important names missing.

I couldn't believe it. I was stuck on a team without *any* of my friends!

Chapter 5

When Counselor Carl finished calling out
the teams, Pia, Jesse, Cole, and Rusty ended up
together on the Orange Team. Lola and Maya
were together on the Green Team. It didn't seem
fair that I had to be all by myself!

Okay, I wasn't all alone. I was with mean
Jennifer, meaner Rory, and a bunch of other kids
that I barely knew. Somehow this wasn't how I'd
imagined this overnight!

"It'll be okay, Amy," Lola said. "It's only for
activities, remember? We'll be together the rest
of the time. We'll still have a blast—you'll see." I
hoped she was right.

When Carl announced that it was time for
lunch, I felt relieved. At least I got to stay with
my friends for a little longer. The counselors
took us back to the log building. Inside was a

big dining room that they called the mess hall. We sat down at long wooden tables. There were sandwiches and chips waiting for us, along with big pitchers of a bright red drink.

"Yum!" Cole said, reaching for the pitcher. "Bug juice!"

"Did you just say *bug* juice?" I asked.

He grinned. "Yup. Bug juice is all you're supposed to drink at camp. Want some?" He poured some into his glass, then pushed the pitcher toward me.

I stared at it, feeling a little queasy. There was a lot I didn't know about camping. But was it possible people actually drank juice made out of *bugs*?

Then Pia giggled. "Don't tease her," she told Cole. "It's okay, Amy. Bug juice is just a silly name. It's really just fruit punch."

Relieved, I took a glass. The juice was watery and sweet—and not a bit buggy-tasting!

After lunch, we divided into our teams for the first activity. The Yellow Team's counselors for that day were Cleo and Cooper. Mrs. Musgrove came along, too. The first thing the counselors did was hand each of us a yellow bandana.

"You can wear them however you like," Cleo said cheerfully. "They'll show your Yellow Team spirit! Whoo-hoo!" She did a little jump and kick.

Jennifer just rolled her eyes.

"Ready to get started?" Cleo asked. "We're going to do an obstacle course!"

She and Cooper led us through the woods on a path that took us to a clearing. I stared at the obstacle course. It was built out of all kinds of natural things—some big logs and stumps, a thick rope tied to a big beam, an overhead ladder made of twisty branches, a long, skinny balance beam built from another log, and some other stuff. I wondered if I'd be able to make it through the course.

"Wow, this looks fun!" Evelyn Najera exclaimed. I didn't know Evelyn very well, but my friends had told me she was the most athletic kid in the fourth grade.

"It *will* be fun," Counselor Cooper said. He was

short and wide with a tanned, friendly face. "Not only that, it will test your outdoor survival skills. For instance, if you ever get lost in the woods, you might need to climb a tree to get a better view so you can figure out where you are . . ."

Cooper spent the next half hour talking about camping and survival skills. It was pretty interesting. I'd never really thought about all the ways you could get in real trouble out in the wilderness. No wonder my parents were a little nervous about me going camping.

Soon it was time to try the obstacle course. "Oh, I almost forgot." Cooper reached into his pocket and pulled out a cute little pin. "Whoever gets through the course the fastest wins one of these."

I was excited when I saw the pin. Maybe I'd win it—I sure was going to try my best!

The counselors called for Evelyn to try the course first. She waited for Cooper's whistle, then raced for the first obstacle—one of the huge logs. Evelyn scrambled over really fast.

Then she ran to the branch ladder and started swinging from rung to rung with ease. After that she did the balance beam, then the log steps, and all the rest.

When she was finished, she jogged over to where we were standing. "That was so cool!" she cried, wiping her brow with her yellow bandana.

"Well done, dear," Mrs. Musgrove said. She had put on a fuzzy orange sweater over her weird outfit. I wasn't surprised. It was a nice day, but definitely not warm enough for shorts.

"Yes, nice job, Evelyn." Cooper made a note on his clipboard. "That time will be tough to beat. Amy Hodges? Why don't you give it a try next?"

"Okay," I said as I walked over to the starting line.

When Cooper blew the whistle, I raced for the first log. But as I started to climb over it, something pricked my hand.

"Ow!" I cried. It felt like the rough bark of the log had given me a splinter!

I stopped and peered at my hand. If it was a splinter, I wanted to get it out right away.

"Amy, what are you doing?" Counselor Cleo called. "Why did you stop?"

"I have a splinter!" I said. "I just want to—"

"Go! Go!" Rory yelled. "The clock is ticking!"

"It's okay, Amy," Evelyn cheered. "You can do it!"

Danny and Yasmin started cheering, too, along with everyone else—except Jennifer.

I wasn't sure what to do. They all seemed to think I should keep going, even with a splinter in my hand! Luckily the splinter was pretty big, and I was able to pull it out easily—even if it hurt a little. The others kept cheering, and Rory was still yelling. So I quickly clambered over the log, then headed for the overhead ladder.

Swinging along hand by hand was a lot harder than it had looked when Evelyn did it, and my hand was sore from the splinter. I barely made it to the last rung. By the time I dropped off, I was huffing and puffing. I'd never had to do anything like this before! I wanted to stop and catch my breath, but I was pretty sure the others wouldn't like that. So I kept going.

The balance beam was next. It looked a lot longer and narrower from close-up. I also noticed there was a big mud puddle beneath it. I climbed up and started across, carefully putting one foot in front of the other.

At first I did okay. But then I caught the toe of my hiking shoe on the beam and almost tripped. I regained my balance just in time to keep from falling forward. But then I started teetering from side to side. Uh-oh! My feet were slipping out from underneath me . . .

I tried to crouch down and grab the beam so I could get my balance again. But it was too late. My feet slipped out from underneath me, and a second later I landed in the muddy puddle with a *splat*! Rory burst out laughing. I felt so embarassed that I wanted to run all the way back to Maple Heights.

Chapter 6

"It's okay, Amy," Counselor Cooper called as I crawled out of the mud. "You did a great job! Jennifer, you're up next."

As Jennifer ran the course, I did my best to wipe the mud off myself. Soon my yellow bandana looked like it should belong to the Brown Team. My new khaki pants were a mess. Pia would probably freak out when she saw them. I felt like crying myself, and not only because my clothes were ruined. So far this camping trip wasn't turning out like I'd expected.

When I finally looked up, Jennifer was about to finish the course. She was moving really quickly and didn't even have a single speck of mud on her! Rory and Yasmin and most of the others made it through the course without any trouble, too.

Danny went last. He was a shy, East Indian kid with glasses. I didn't know him very well, since he was in Mrs. Musgrove's class. He went a lot slower than some of the others, but he made it all the way through, too. He finished by crawling carefully over the final log and then standing up and brushing off his jeans.

"Awesome job, people!" Counselor Cleo exclaimed. "Let's see . . ." She checked her clipboard and compared all of our times. "Looks like Evelyn has the fastest time. Evelyn, you win the pin!" Cleo clapped her hands and did a little cheerleader jump.

Cooper handed Evelyn her pin. "Everyone ready to clean up for dinner and then s'mores?" he asked.

Most of the kids cheered. But I groaned.

"Some more?" I muttered, glancing over at the obstacle course—especially that stupid mud puddle. "Please don't tell me we have to do *that* again!"

Jennifer heard what I said and shot me a look. Lola calls it Jennifer's "you smell like feet" look.

"Was that supposed to be a joke?" Jennifer asked. "Because it really wasn't that funny."

"What do you mean?" I asked. I hadn't been trying to make a joke.

Jennifer was already walking away. I shrugged.

But now Rory was staring at me. He pointed one finger at me, almost touching my nose. There was tons of dirt under his fingernails, even though he hadn't fallen in the mud like I had. In fact, he'd done every part of the obstacle course perfectly.

"Are you *clueless*?" he demanded. "Don't you know what a *s'more* is?"

I wanted to push his finger away, but I was too scared. He was the biggest ten-year-old on earth. So instead, I just took a step backward and mumbled, "Don't call me clueless."

"I call it like I see it, Amy *Hodgepodge*," he said. "And if you don't know what a s'more is, that means you're clueless."

I frowned. I love it when my friends call me Amy Hodgepodge. It makes me feel special. But hearing Rory say it was different. Now it sounded like an insult.

I wanted to shout out "I think you're clueless!"

but I stayed quiet and headed back toward the tents. I tried to shake off what had just happened with Rory. Maybe once I was back with my friends, this trip would start being fun again.

Lola and Maya were already in the tent when I got there. "Amy!" Lola cried when she saw me. "What happened to you?"

I sighed and kicked off my muddy shoes. "Don't ask."

Lola shrugged. "Okay. But check it out—Maya won a pin for being the best paddler in canoeing!"

"It's not that big a deal," Maya said with a bashful smile. She tugged at her green bandana, which was draped around her neck. There was a cute leaf-shaped pin on it now. "I just tried my best, that's all."

"That's great, Maya." I dug into my duffel bag, pulling out clean clothes to change into before dinner. "Anyway, canoeing sounds like a lot more fun than the obstacle course I had to do." I glanced around. "Where are Jesse and Pia?"

"They should be here soon," Lola said. "We

heard the Orange Team went out in the woods on a scavenger hunt."

"That sounds cool. Oh, I was wondering," I said. "What's a s'more?"

Lola looked surprised. "You don't know what a s'more is?"

I shook my head. She wasn't saying it to be mean like Jennifer and Rory. But I still felt kind of dumb. Everyone seemed to know about s'mores except for me. I guess it was one of the many things my parents and grandparents had forgotten to tell me about when I was homeschooled.

"Ooh, they're so good!" Maya's big green eyes lit up. "First you toast a marshmallow over the fire until it's all warm and tan and squishy. Then you put it on a graham cracker with a piece of chocolate so it gets all gooey."

Lola licked her lips. "Uh-huh. And you put another graham cracker on top to make a little sandwich. The warm marshmallow melts the chocolate. It's totally yum. And you'll want some more and s'more and s'more!"

"That does sound good," I said. "I can't wait to try one!"

"Stick 'em up, everybody!" Rusty leaped into the tent. His orange bandana was tied across his mouth and nose like an old-fashioned bandit.

Cole was right behind him. He was wearing his bandana around his upper arm. "Hey," he greeted us.

Lola frowned at her twin brother. "Are you supposed to be over here in the girls' camp?" she demanded. "Anyway, how did you know we wouldn't be in the middle of changing clothes in here or something?"

"You aren't, are you?" Cole said with a shrug. "So what's the big deal?"

"How was the scavenger hunt?" Maya asked them.

The two boys grinned at each other. "Oh, it was . . . interesting," Cole said.

"Yeah. Very, very interesting," Rusty added, yanking his bandana down so it hung around his neck. Then they both laughed.

I glanced at Lola and Maya. They looked as confused as I was. Lola shrugged.

"Whatever," she said. "Where are Jesse and Pia?"

"Here we are." Pia hurried in. Her orange bandana looked totally stylish with her striped hoodie and tan pants. As soon as she saw me, she gasped. "Amy!" she cried. "What happened to your outfit?"

"It fell into a mud puddle along with the rest of me." I grimaced. "My team had to do an obstacle course. It was really hard. I tripped and fell off the balance beam into a giant mud puddle!" I didn't bother to tell them I was the *only* one who had fallen in the mud.

Jesse was a few steps behind Pia. She was staring back over her shoulder with a nervous look on her face. For a second I was worried. Was there a bear creeping into the tent or something?

I glanced out the door flap. No bears.

"Hi, Jesse," I said. "Did you have fun on the scavenger hunt?"

She shrugged. "It was okay."

That was all she said, which was kind of weird. Jesse *loves* to talk. She always has plenty to say about everything. But now, she just peered at her bunk and then went to sit down.

"Look out, Jesse!" Cole cried suddenly. "There's a huge spider on your bed!"

Jesse shrieked and jumped away. Then the boys started laughing.

Lola glanced over at Jesse's bed. "There's no spider," she said. "They're just being dumb."

Jesse glared at the boys. For some reason, that made them laugh even harder.

Pia sighed. "Give it a rest, you guys," she told Cole and Rusty. Then she looked at Lola, Maya, and me. "They've been teasing Jesse all afternoon. She's, um, a little nervous about being in the woods."

"The other times I camped, we were at a campsite at the beach in Florida." Jesse looked miserable. "There were only a few palm trees there. Not, you know, deep woods. Like this." She glanced out the tent door and shivered.

"Yeah," Rusty said. "She's afraid a vicious twig might get her."

"Or a bloodthirsty bird." Cole grinned. "Did you see her jump when that robin flew across the trail?"

The boys laughed again. But I felt bad for Jesse. It seemed I wasn't the only one who wasn't having the best time in the wilderness.

Lola chased the boys out of the tent so I could change my clothes. A few minutes later we met everyone back at the mess hall. While we ate, Counselor Chill gave a talk. Chill looked and sounded like a surfer dude, with his floppy blond hair and laid-back voice. But he knew a ton about nature and camping. He talked about using shadows and landmarks to find your way in the woods, and then started telling us about some of the local birds and plants. I listened with interest, but not everyone was paying attention. Jennifer and her friends whispered and giggled the whole time he was talking. They didn't stop until Mrs. Clark went over and reprimanded them.

After dinner and showers we all headed to Campfire Clearing. A huge fire was burning in the fire pit. It was getting cooler as the sun set. On the walk over I was chilly even though I was wearing my down jacket. But it was nice and warm near the fire.

Jesse had talked a lot at dinner, and even got in an argument with the boys about which was better, chocolate chip cookies or oatmeal raisin. She'd seemed almost like her usual self. But now she looked nervous again. "Why do we have to sit around outside in the dark, anyway?" she mumbled. "Is that really anyone's idea of fun?"

"Sure," Rusty said. "The werewolves that hide in the woods love it."

Cole snorted with laughter. "Yeah. The one-eyed monsters, too."

"You guys are *so* funny," Pia said as she glared at the boys.

"Leave her alone," Lola added. "Don't be such dorks."

Just then, Counselor Chill came toward us carrying a big tray. "Help yourselves, dudes," he said. His tray had a big bowl of marshmallows on one side, and a bunch of long, wooden sticks on the other. They looked sort of like giant chopsticks.

"Cool." Pia grabbed a stick and a handful of marshmallows. "Come on, Jesse. Toasting marshmallows will make you feel better."

My friends showed me how to poke a marshmallow onto the end of my stick, then hold it over the edge of the fire. At first I held mine way too far away from the fire.

"It will never get brown if you don't hold it closer." Cole stuck his stick farther into the fire until it was almost touching a flame. "See?"

He pulled back his stick. His marshmallow was the same shade of tan as Pia's pants. When he pulled it off the stick, it looked gooey and delicious. He blew on it to cool it off, then popped it into his mouth.

"Hey!" Lola said. "You're supposed to make it into a s'more. Counselor Coco is coming around with the stuff now, see?" She pointed.

"That one was just a test." Cole was already reaching for another marshmallow. "This will be the real one."

I giggled. Finally everyone was getting along again. Now, if only I could get my marshmallow to turn out like Cole's . . .

I pulled my stick out of the fire, but my

marshmallow was still white. When I touched it,
it barely felt warm.

I stuck it back toward the fire. This time I
held it closer to the flames. Then closer. Then
even a little closer . . .

WHOOMP!

"Oh, no!" I cried, yanking the stick back. But it was too late. My marshmallow was on fire!

"Uh-oh, Amy has the first char-mallow!" Rusty cried.

"Blow it out!" Maya grabbed my stick and began blowing on the burning marshmallow. Thankfully, the flames went right out.

She handed it back to me. Now it was all black and charred—definitely not something I would want to eat. I felt my earlier gloominess creep back. Wasn't anything going to be easy for me on this wilderness trip? Maybe Rory was right . . . I was clueless.

Chapter 7

Maya yawned as she climbed into her bed. "It's still early, but I'm ready for sleep," she said. "Camping is tiring."

Pia was folding her clothes. We had all changed into our pajamas. Everyone's were pretty normal, but of course Pia's pajamas made a fashion statement. Hers were pink with sparkly beads on the cuffs.

"I know," Pia said. "I think I—" She broke off with a gasp.

"What's wrong?" Lola asked.

"Th-there," Pia stammered. She pointed at the side of the tent.

I was almost afraid to turn around. But I couldn't stand not looking, either. What if it was a huge spider on the tent wall? Or maybe a bat had flown inside . . .

I spun around—and saw a big, creepy-looking shadow on the side of the tent. It looked like a monster was lurking just outside!

"What is that?" Jesse shrieked.

"Oh my gosh," cried Maya.

"Hold on a second," Lola said calmly. She got up and went over to the tent door.

"Lola, be careful!" Jesse squeaked.

Lola stuck her head out the door. "Okay, you guys," she yelled. "You can come out now."

The sound of familiar laughter came from outside. I let out a big breath.

"It's only Cole and Rusty!" Pia said. "Those knuckleheads!"

Maya laughed. "They really got us this time."

"Yeah," I agreed with a smile.

But Jesse didn't say anything. She just crawled into her bed and turned toward the wall.

"Jesse?" Maya said. "Are you okay? It was only a prank."

Jesse didn't answer.

"Where are the boys?" I asked Lola when she

came back into the tent a moment later.

"They spotted Counselor Cookie coming this way and took off," Lola said. "We'll have to get back at them tomorrow." Then she noticed how Jesse was in bed and facing the wall. "Hey, Jesse," she added. "You okay? It was just a stupid prank. You know—typical sneaky boys."

Jesse still didn't answer. She didn't even turn around or say anything when Counselor Cookie stuck her head in to make sure we were all in bed.

"Maybe we should all get some sleep," Maya suggested softly after the counselor left.

Nobody had any better ideas. So we did just that.

❀ ❀ ❀

"Okay, everyone grab a partner," Counselor Coco said.

It was the second day of the trip. Breakfast had ended a few minutes earlier. Now I was standing at the canoe dock with the rest of the Yellow Team.

"Danny, you're my partner," Rory said quickly,

and then looked in my direction. "I don't want to get stuck in a canoe with some dumb girl."

Evelyn rolled her eyes. Then she looked at Yasmin. "Want to be partners?" she asked.

I looked around. The other kids were pairing off fast. Before I knew it, there was only one partner left for me. Jennifer.

I bit my lip. But there wasn't much I could do about it now. So I decided to try to make the best of things.

"I guess that makes us partners," I told her as cheerfully as I could.

She rolled her eyes. "Duh," she said. "I hope you know how to paddle. I want to win the pin today."

"Um, actually, I've never gone canoeing before," I said.

Jennifer frowned. "Let me guess. They don't teach that in homeschool. Figures!"

I wasn't sure what to say to that. "Come on," I mumbled. "Let's get our safety vests on."

Coco helped us pick out vests and paddles. Then we pushed our canoe into the water.

Jennifer already seemed to know all about canoeing. I thought that might make things easier. But it actually made it harder. She wasn't very patient. Every time I accidentally moved my paddle in the wrong direction, she yelled at me. That made me nervous, and then I messed up even more.

"Quit it!" she yelled after the third or fourth time I moved my paddle forward instead of backward. "You're making us go in circles!"

"Sorry." I tried to fix my mistake by moving my paddle the other way. Unfortunately, now Jennifer was moving *her* paddle the other way, trying to move us forward. We started turning in circles in the other direction! It made me feel kind of dizzy.

"What's wrong with you, anyway?" Jennifer exclaimed, jabbing her paddle into the water to stop the boat from turning. We had drifted so close to shore by now that her paddle hit the bottom of the lake.

"Look, I'm trying my best," I said. "If you

just tell me how to do it instead of yelling so much, I might get better at this."

"I'm not getting paid to teach canoeing lessons," she said. She shoved her paddle into the water again and tried to push us away from shore.

But my paddle was still in the water. It had gotten stuck on a rock or something.

"Wait!" I cried. "I need to pull my paddle out first."

Jennifer didn't answer. She just pushed harder against the bottom of the lake. I felt the paddle slip out of my hands. It was still stuck under the rock, so it disappeared underwater.

"Hey!" I cried. "Hold on, I dropped my paddle!" I leaned over the side of the canoe and tried to reach for it.

All of a sudden, Jennifer shouted, "Stop it, Amy! Don't do that!"

I was tired of listening to her. Since she yelled no matter what I did I figured I might as well do what I wanted. So I leaned a little farther. My fingertips touched the handle of the paddle. I almost had it . . .

"Aaaah!" Jennifer cried.

The canoe tipped to the side. "Whoa!" I yelled. I tried to straighten up, but it was too late. It rolled all the way over.

We both jumped out of the canoe just in time to avoid getting completely dunked, but we were left standing in cold water that came up to our knees.

"Now look what you did!" Jennifer screamed. Her face was bright red. "You can't do anything right!"

Counselor Coco had been busy watching one of the other pairs. But now she hurried over. "What's going on over here?" she called, sounding worried.

"Jennifer, darling, is everything all right?"

Jennifer's mom added from the dock. She had just wandered out there holding a cell phone.

"Aargh!" Jennifer exclaimed. "People who don't know anything about camping shouldn't come on this trip! If anyone cares, I'm going back to my tent to get dry pants and shoes." She stomped through the water onto shore. Her mother wandered after her with her cell phone pressed to her ear.

"Are you okay, Amy?" Coco held out a hand to help me up the bank.

"I'm fine," I said.

Coco helped me pull the canoe back onto shore. Meanwhile Evelyn and Yasmin paddled over to see what was happening.

"I guess I'm not much good at canoeing," I told them.

"Don't worry about it, Amy," Coco said. "You did great for your first time."

"Yeah. Don't let Jennifer get to you," Evelyn added, and Yasmin nodded.

I smiled weakly. It was nice of them to try to make me feel better. Too bad it wasn't working.

Chapter 8

I waited for my friends outside the mess hall for lunch. "See you after lunch, Stanley," Maya said as the Green Team arrived and then split up to sit with their friends.

When Stanley hurried off into the hall, she sighed. "I feel badly for him," she said.

Lola nodded. "Yeah. Me too. Some kids were teasing him because he barely found any of the things on the scavenger hunt," she told me.

"You two should feel badly for *me*," I said. "I got stuck with Jennifer as a canoeing partner."

I told them the whole story as we walked inside. We found a seat as far away from Jennifer and her friends as possible. Our sandwiches and drinks were already set out for us.

"It sounds like it was Jennifer's fault you tipped over," Lola said.

"I guess it was both our faults," I admitted. "But she blamed me for the whole thing."

Just then the Orange Team arrived. Pia, Jesse, and the boys hurried to our table.

"Don't be mad, Jesse," Cole was saying when they got there. "We were just kidding around."

"What happened?" Lola asked.

"Cole and Rusty keep teasing Jesse about being scared," Pia said, frowning at the boys. "They won't leave her alone."

For a second Lola looked really mad. I thought she was going to yell at Cole and Rusty.

But then she just shrugged. "Hey, Jesse, did you ever hear the legend of the Beast of Camp Falling Leaf?"

Wait a second! Why was Lola helping the boys tease Jesse? That didn't make any sense . . . or seem very nice.

"N-no," said Jesse as she looked at Lola suspiciously. I couldn't blame Jesse. I was suspicious, too.

"It's this huge, shaggy monster," Lola said.

"Kind of like Bigfoot, only scarier. It's said to roam the woods around here."

Maya shot Jesse a worried look. "Really?" she said. "I've never heard of it."

"Yeah. And there's only one way to survive if you run into it," Lola said in a spooky voice. She wrapped her arms around herself tightly. "You have to curl yourself into a tiny ball on the ground. You know—so the beast won't think that you're a threat to it."

The boys were listening, too. "Then it will leave you alone?" Rusty asked.

She shook her head. "Nope. It might still eat you—*unless . . .*"

"Unless what?" Pia asked breathlessly.

"Unless you immediately yell 'Inkle, dinkle, dattle!' three times as loudly as you can."

Cole laughed. "Good one, sis!" he said. "Inkle, dinkle, dattle. Better remember that just in case, huh, Jesse?"

Jesse stared down at her food and didn't answer. I felt bad for her. And I was also kind of disappointed in Lola. I thought she would want to help Jesse feel better, not try to scare her even more.

"I have to go to the latrine," Jesse said. She stood up and grabbed Maya by the arm. "Will you come with me? I don't want to go by myself."

"Sure." Maya got up, and the two of them left.

"Great story, Lola," Rusty said. "Did you just make it up, or have you been saving it for the right time?"

Lola shrugged. "I didn't make it up," she said, picking up her sandwich. "It's true."

Cole rolled his eyes. "Yeah, right."

"So how was the scavenger hunt?" Pia asked Lola. I guessed she was trying to change the subject before Jesse got back.

It worked. We talked about our activities and other stuff for the rest of lunch. Afterward it was time to divide up again for our final team activity.

"Everyone ready for a supercool scavenger hunt?" Chill asked when the Yellow Team gathered outside. He and Cookie were our counselors for this activity.

Everyone cheered, including me. A scavenger hunt sounded like a lot more fun than canoeing or an obstacle course. The counselors led our team to a clearing off to one side of the mess hall and passed out lists of stuff that could be found in the woods. We were told to find as many items from the list as we could. Each of our names was written on a sign tacked to a tree around the edges of the clearing. We were supposed to come back and drop off what we'd found by our names so we wouldn't have to carry everything the whole time.

"Ready?" Cookie asked.

"Okay, dudes—go for it!" Chill cried.

I took off into the woods with the others. The scavenger hunt reminded me of activities I'd done for homeschooling, like the time Obaasan had taken me to the museum and asked me to find at least five works of art with dogs in them. Maybe I would finally be good at something on this trip—and I could win one of those cool leaf pins!

Things started off pretty well. The first three items on the list were easy to find—a yellow leaf, a pinecone, and a Y-shaped twig. I found all three right away.

Those three things were pretty small, so I decided to carry them as I searched for the rest of the items on the list. I pulled the list out of my pocket. I read it while I hurried down a winding trail. "Okay, a red berry. I think I can—oof!"

Since I wasn't paying attention, my foot got caught on a tree root, and I tripped. I landed flat on my face.

"Ugh," I said, sitting up. I wasn't hurt, but my pinecone was squashed.

At least nobody was around to see me being so clumsy. I checked the pocket where I carried the compass my dad had bought me. Luckily, it hadn't broken in the fall.

Then I headed back to where I'd found the first pinecone. When I bent to pick up a new one, I noticed something white lying in the leaves nearby. I squinted. Was it a mushroom, or maybe a light-colored stone? No, it didn't quite look like either of those things . . .

I poked at it with the toe of my shoe. When I got a better look, I gasped. It was a small, delicate-looking piece of bone—just like the dinosaur skull fossils I'd seen at the Natural History museum! I had found something way better than all the things on the list—I had found a dinosaur fossil!

Chapter 9

"Oh my gosh!" I cried, carefully picking up the bone. It was smooth and pale and looked super-old, as if it had been lying there in the woods forever. I held it in the hem of my shirt so I wouldn't get fingerprints on it. I'd seen that once on a TV show about fossils.

I ran back to the clearing, being careful not to trip again. I definitely didn't want to break *this*! Maybe I could sell it to a museum for thousands of dollars!

Counselors Chill and Cookie were waiting for us in the middle of the clearing. A few of the other kids were nearby, dropping things off underneath their names.

"Slow down, Amy Hodgepodge," Rory said. "Too bad you didn't go this fast on that obstacle course yesterday."

I wasn't going to let his teasing bother me now. "You'd be in a hurry, too, if you'd found this," I exclaimed. "I'm pretty sure it's a dinosaur skull!"

"A dinosaur?" Evelyn sounded doubtful. "But it's so small."

"Some dinosaurs were tiny, like the size of a chicken," I explained. "I did a whole

homeschooling unit on fossils last year."

"What is it, Amy?" Chill asked, wandering over to us with Cookie right behind him. "Is everything okay?"

"Look what I just found!" I exclaimed, carefully holding up my treasure. "Can you believe it? I think it might be a dinosaur fossil!"

Chill stepped closer and peered at it. "Not exactly," he said with a chuckle. "Cool find, though. Looks to be a squirrel skull."

"Nice try, Amy!" Cookie said with a laugh. "It's a good thing our nature expert Chill is here. If it had really been a dinosaur bone, you would have won that pin for sure!"

A squirrel skull? Yuck. I dropped it on the ground and kicked it out of the way, feeling super-embarrassed.

When I wandered off toward the woods, I saw Jennifer and Rory smirking at me. My heart sank as I realized they had seen the whole thing.

"Yeah, nice try," she said as they passed by me. Rory laughed and picked up a stick. "Look!

It's a dinosaur tail!" he said, imitating me.

"Now that the counselors know how clueless you are, they'll probably be afraid to let you out of your tent again. Who knows what kind of trouble you could get into," added Jennifer.

I ignored them and dumped the pinecone and other stuff in my spot. Suddenly the scavenger hunt didn't seem like much fun anymore.

Still, I figured I might as well keep at it. I headed back into the woods. On the way, I noticed Evelyn and Danny standing nearby. Evelyn had a pretty loud voice. I heard her say something about being surprised I came on the trip.

"I can't believe that Amy actually came on this trip," Evelyn was saying in a loud voice. "I can't believe that someone can be so clueless about camping," she continued.

Danny laughed. I felt my face go hot, and I turned to walk in the opposite direction. It was bad enough to have mean people like Jennifer and Rory tease me. But now it seemed like even some of the nicer kids thought I was in over my head on this camping trip. Were they right? Should I have listened to my parents and stayed at home?

I was so upset that I didn't try very hard to find the rest of the items on the list. By the end of the scavenger hunt, I only had seven things in my pile. Yasmin had all fifteen, so she won the pin.

It was time to go back to the tent to get ready for dinner. I walked slowly, still thinking about everything. When I entered the tent, Lola and Maya were changing their shoes. Pia was checking her hair in a hand mirror. Jesse was zipping open her suitcase, which was sitting on her bunk.

"Hi, Amy," Pia greeted me, looking up from her mirror. "How was the scavenger hunt?"

"Okay," I said glumly.

Maya glanced over in surprise. "What's the matter, Amy?" she asked. "You sound kind of bummed out."

I shrugged. "I guess maybe camping isn't as much fun as I thought it would be."

"Oh, Amy . . ." Lola began. But before she

could say anything else, Jesse suddenly let out a loud scream.

"What's going on?" Pia cried, almost dropping her mirror. "What's wrong?"

We all rushed to Jesse's side. As soon as I looked down at her open suitcase, I realized what had happened. Lying there on top of her pajamas was a huge snake!

Chapter 10

It only took a moment for us to figure out that the snake was fake. It was pretty realistic-looking, though.

"Those sneaky boys!" Jesse said as she clenched her fists.

I bit my lip. Jesse seemed sure that Cole and Rusty were behind this prank. But were they? After all, they were nowhere in sight. And Lola was right here with us . . .

"Are you sure it wasn't one of *us* who did it?" I blurted out, looking over at Lola.

Maya blinked in surprise. "One of us?" she said.

"What are you trying to say, Amy?" Lola demanded.

I wished I could take back what I had said.

"Um, I was just remembering how Lola told

that scary story at lunch, and, well . . . I'm sorry, Lola! I know it wasn't you. Please don't be mad." My eyes filled with tears. On top of everything else that had gone wrong on this trip, I couldn't stand it if my dumb comment made one of my best friends mad at me, too.

To my surprise, Lola smiled. "Good," she said. "I guess if Amy suspects me, it means my plan must be working."

"Huh?" Jesse narrowed her eyes. "You mean she's right? You are trying to scare me?"

"No way," Lola said. "Do you really think I'd play such a lame prank?"

Pia picked up the rubber snake with two fingers. "I certainly hope not," she said.

Lola shook her head. "It definitely must have been the boys. But don't worry, I already figured out the perfect way to get back at them for being so rotten to Jesse." She smiled at me. "Maybe it'll even show Amy that camping can be fun after all."

I smiled back. "That sounds good to me."

Jesse looked impatient. "So what are you

waiting for?" she demanded. For the first time since we got to camp, she sounded more like her old bossy self. "Tell us the plan!"

"Okay," Lola said. "It's like this . . ."

❀ ❀ ❀

"Bed check," Counselor Cookie sang out, sticking her head into our tent. "Everyone snug as a bug in a rug?"

Maya giggled. "I don't know," she said. "How snug is a bug in a rug, exactly?"

That made us all laugh, including Cookie. Once she made sure we were in bed, she said good night and left.

We had already turned out the lights. It was pretty dark in the tent, but the moon shining through the tree branches outside made pretty patterns on the canvas ceiling. I stared at the shadows and thought about how the day had gone. Dinner with my friends had been fun. I'd also enjoyed singing campfire songs at Campfire Clearing afterward, even though I couldn't help noticing that everybody else seemed to know most of the songs already, while I'd just stumbled along.

I guess camping isn't quite what I thought it would be, I told myself.

"Psst! Amy," Lola whispered from below. "Ready to go?"

I immediately sat up and pushed back the covers. I was still dressed in my jeans and hiking boots.

"I'm ready," I whispered back to Lola. Before I climbed down from my bunk, I grabbed my windup lantern from the shelf. It was time to put Lola's plan into action!

Soon all five of us were sneaking along a path in the woods. Lola was carrying a blanket. I was carrying my lantern, but I kept it off so the counselors wouldn't see us.

It was kind of scary being outside after dark. There were lots of nighttime noises that I had never heard before. At first I was afraid Jesse would be too scared to make it to the boys' tents. I wasn't even sure *I* was going to make it! But luckily, Pia had been to camp and she recognized all the strange sounds. It was a lot less scary once we could all identify them as crickets, frogs, or owls, and not ghosts and monsters.

Finally we reached the boys' tents. They were set up in a row along a stream. Lola pointed to the tent at one end of the line.

"That one's theirs," she whispered. "Let's get 'em!"

We all knew what we were supposed to do. I handed Lola my lantern. She and Jesse tiptoed off in one direction, while I went the other way with Pia and Maya. The three of us found a good hiding spot behind a clump of bushes near the boys' tent.

"Let's all count to fifty to give Lola and Jesse time to get into position," Pia whispered into my ear. "As soon as they hear us start, they'll start, too."

I nodded and started counting in my head. When I reached fifty, I looked at the others. They both nodded and grinned.

"One, two, three . . ." Maya whispered.

Then we all let loose. We howled and shrieked and moaned as loudly as we could.

It only took a second before we heard sleepy,

confused voices from inside the tent. Cole and Rusty stumbled out, rubbing their eyes and looking around.

That was when a huge, dark figure with a single glowing eye stomped toward them with its arms outstretched! It was taller than the tallest counselor and horribly lumpy.

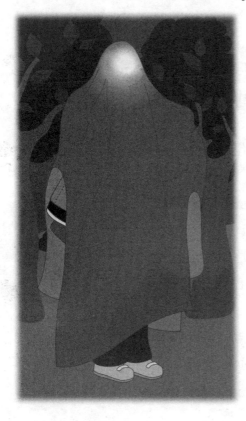

"Grrrrrrrrrr!" it growled as it staggered closer and closer to Cole and Rusty. "ROWRRRRRR!"

Chapter 11

The monster looked pretty scary, even though I knew it was only Jesse sitting on Lola's shoulders with the blanket draped over them and my lantern blinking through the fabric. But the boys *didn't* know that, and they were totally terrified!

"It's the Beast of Camp Falling Leaf!" Rusty yelled frantically.

Cole jumped backward so quickly that he almost tripped over his own feet.

A second later they were both on the ground, curled into tight little balls. "Inkle, dinkle, dattle! Inkle, dinkle, dattle! Inkle, dinkle, dattle!" they cried out in loud, shaky voices.

Meanwhile Stanley and Danny stumbled out of the tent after them, yawning and looking confused. "What's going on out here?" Stanley asked.

Then the Beast of Camp Falling Leaf started laughing. Suddenly Cole opened his eyes and looked up.

"Lola?" he asked suspiciously.

Jesse threw back the blanket to reveal herself sitting on Lola's shoulders. "Gotcha!" she cried, sliding down.

Stanley laughed. "Hey, that's pretty good!" he cried. Danny laughed, too. So did Pia, Maya, and I as we hurried out from our hiding spot.

Rusty sat up and brushed the dirt off his shirt. "Hey! That's not funny!" he cried.

"Yeah!" Cole agreed.

"Well, if you ask me, I think it was pretty funny," said Stanley.

"Me too," said Lola.

"Now you two know what it feels like to be scared," Jesse added while glaring at Rusty and Cole.

Both boys grinned guiltily. "Oh, okay. You got us this time," said Cole. Rusty nodded in agreement.

"Does this mean you've learned your lesson?" Lola demanded, crossing her arms over her chest. "And don't you have something to say to Jesse?"

"I'm listening," Jesse said with a smirk.

Cole sighed loudly. "All right," he said. "I'm sorry, Jesse. I guess we got carried away."

"Yeah," Rusty added. "I'm sorry, too."

"Psst! I think I just heard Counselor Carl coming this way," Stanley hissed. "Come on, let's get back to bed before he catches us!"

❀ ❀ ❀

The next morning after breakfast, it was

time for the big nature walk. "I'm really glad we're all together for our last activity," Lola said as we walked along a wooded path with the rest of the group. Counselor Chill was in the lead. He was telling us all about everything from why leaves change colors in the fall to stuff about the position of the sun to the names of the plants, trees, birds, insects, and everything we were seeing.

"Me too," I agreed. "This is fun! And Chill knows a ton about nature." I remembered the talks he'd given at some of our meals, and how quickly he'd identified that squirrel skull.

"Really?" Rusty grinned and glanced at the counselor. "Because he looks like all he knows about is surfing, *dude.*"

Pia rolled her eyes. "Come on, we're falling behind. I can't hear what he's saying."

She, Lola, Maya, and the boys hurried to catch up. But I hung back. I'd just seen a pretty black-and-white bird in a tree nearby and wanted a better look.

"What's that?" Jesse asked, stopping with me.

"A woodpecker. See the red spot on his head? My grandfather taught me all about birds. He says the best thing about moving halfway across the country is that he gets to learn about a whole new bunch of birds."

While we watched the woodpecker hop up and down the tree trunk, the rest of the group kept going. The only person still behind us was Stanley.

"Is everything okay, Stanley?" I asked.

He limped toward us. "Um, not exactly," he admitted. "I twisted my ankle on a root a few minutes ago."

"Oh, no!" Jesse said. "We'd better tell Chill."

"No!" Stanley blurted out. His face turned red. "I mean, I should be okay."

"You don't look okay," Jesse said.

He shrugged. "I don't want the other kids to know. People have been teasing me because I've never been camping before."

My eyes widened. "You haven't?" I said.

"Neither have I! I thought I was the only one."

He smiled at me. "Me too."

"Well, we still have to get you help," Jesse declared. "Hey, you guys, wait up!" she called.

Most of the group had already disappeared around a curve. Only Jennifer, Rory, and Evelyn were still in view. All three heard Jesse and stopped.

"What's the problem?" Rory asked. "Did the shoelaces come untied on Stanley's nerd shoes?"

Jesse frowned at him. "Don't be so mean," she said. "Stanley hurt his ankle. We need to tell Chill so we can go back to camp."

"Are you kidding?" Jennifer frowned. "I don't want to go back now. We're right in the middle of the nature walk."

Evelyn looked at Stanley's leg. "I twisted my ankle running track last year. It really hurt."

"We need to get him to the camp nurse," Jesse said. "Let's get the others so we can go back." It was good to hear Jesse be her normal bossy self again, but I wondered if part of why she wanted to turn back was to get out of the spooky woods sooner. Either way, it didn't matter. The important thing was helping Stanley get to the nurse.

"Rory, why don't you let Stanley lean on you so he can walk faster," I suggested.

Rory stepped back. "Ew, no way," he said. "You do it."

"I have a better idea," Evelyn said. "We can wait here with Stanley, and Jennifer can run and tell Chill what happened."

"Why don't you do it?" Jennifer said. "You're the one who likes running so much."

Jesse sighed loudly. "Look, we're just wasting time," she complained. "Come on, Evelyn. You and I can help Stanley walk, and we'll all go tell Chill."

"Fine, whatever," Jennifer muttered.

She and Rory walked ahead while Jesse and Evelyn supported Stanley. I carried Jesse and Evelyn's water bottles and watched for roots and rocks in the trail so Stanley wouldn't trip again.

We walked that way for a few minutes. It was slow going. Still, I expected us to catch up with the group soon.

"Where are they?" Jesse asked after a while. "I can't even hear anyone anymore."

"I guess we spent more time arguing with each other than I thought," Evelyn said.

I stopped walking and listened for the sound of our group. But all I could hear were the birds twittering in the trees and the cool autumn breeze rustling the dried leaves.

"Well, we'll catch up sooner or later," I said.

"All we have to do is follow the trail."

Suddenly Jennifer stopped short and pointed ahead. "Are you sure about that?" she said. "Look, the trail splits up there."

Sure enough, there was a fork in the trail. One branch went off to the left, and the other wound around to the right.

"Which way do you think they went?" Jesse asked worriedly.

Rory stepped toward the right-hand trail. "They went this way," he said. "I can tell. There are some broken twigs and stuff there, see?"

"I see," I said. "But it looks like there are also broken twigs going the other way, too."

But Rory was already hurrying down the right-hand trail and the others were following. I shrugged and did the same.

We walked for a few minutes, but didn't catch up to the group. "We should have found them by now." Jesse's voice shook a little. "I think we went the wrong way."

Rory frowned. "No big deal," he said. "We'll

just cut through the woods here." He pointed to
the left. "We'll come to the other trail that way."
He started pushing his way through the trees
and brush.

"Are you sure this is a good idea?" Stanley
asked. He sounded tired. I bet his ankle hurt a lot.

"Quit complaining," Jennifer snapped.

"You're the reason we're lost in the first place."

"We're not lost," Rory called back. "I know which way to go."

But he was wrong again. After a few more minutes, there was still no sign of the other trail. Worse yet, none of us had kept track of which way we'd come from in the first place, so we couldn't even go back to the original trail.

"What are we going to do now?" Jesse cried. Her voice was really shaking now. "We're lost in the woods!"

Chapter 12

"This is all your fault!" Jennifer snapped at Rory.

"I didn't see *you* trying to help!" Rory shot back. Jesse wrapped her arms around herself. "This is sooo bad! What if we get so lost they never find us?" she cried. I could tell she was starting to panic.

For a second I wanted to panic, too.

Then I remembered Obaasan's words: *think positively*. That made me feel a little braver.

"Hold on, everyone!" I called out. "I have an idea. Just listen to me for a second, okay?"

"Why should we listen to *you*?" Jennifer said. "You've never even been camping before."

"Because I paid attention to our lectures. And because I have *this*." I reached into my pocket and pulled out my compass. Just as I had promised my dad, I had kept the compass in my pocket for the entire trip.

Rory frowned. "What good will that do us? We don't know what direction the others went."

"But we do know which way camp is," I said.

"We do?" Stanley asked.

I smiled and nodded. "Don't you remember? When we left, we were walking right into the sun."

Evelyn nodded. "That's true," she agreed. "I squinted the whole first half hour."

"Counselor Chill said in the morning the sun rises in the east, so that means we were going east," I said. "So if we go west—the opposite of east—we should find our way back to camp."

Stanley looked impressed. "Wow, Amy. I thought you said you didn't know anything about camping!"

"I didn't." I smiled back. "But I'm a fast learner."

"I think it's a stupid plan," said Jennifer.

"Yeah," Rory agreed. "It'll never work."

Jesse shrugged. "Fine. You two can go whichever way you want."

"We'll be sure to send a search party after you when we get back to camp." Evelyn giggled.

I checked the compass. "This way," I said, pointing west.

Evelyn, Jesse, and Stanley followed me right away. After a few moments Rory and Jennifer came along, too, grumbling the whole time.

After walking and following my compass for a while, we finally stepped out of the woods into Campfire Clearing. "We did it!" Jesse cried.

"You mean *Amy* did it," Stanley corrected.

"Hooray for Amy," Evelyn exclaimed.

Everyone was so relieved. Even Rory was smiling. "I guess you're not as clueless as I thought, Amy Hodgepodge."

I smiled at him. For Rory, that was almost an

apology. "Thanks, Rory."

Jennifer didn't say anything. But I thought she looked at least a teensy-bit impressed as she glared at me.

We hurried to the main building and found Mrs. Clark. When she heard what had happened, she took Stanley to the nurse and asked the other counselors to call Chill on the walkie-talkie to tell him we were safe.

A little while later the whole group returned to camp. "Amy, we heard what you did!" Pia cried, rushing over and giving me a hug.

"Yeah, you're a hero!" Lola agreed with a grin.

"Good job!" Maya added. "We were so worried when we noticed you guys were missing!"

Counselor Cooper came over just in time to hear them. "You're right, girls," he said. "Amy is a hero. That's why the other counselors and I agreed she deserves this."

He held up a leaf-shaped pin. It was like the reward pins, except it was twice as big.

"It's Camp Falling Leaf's biggest prize,"

Cooper told me. "The Best Camper award."

"Thanks," I said shyly, accepting the pin. It was beautiful!

I couldn't help feeling proud of myself. I might not be good at everything about camping. But that's okay. I was good at something when it really mattered.

"What do you think, Amy?" Pia asked as she helped me attach my new pin to my sweatshirt. "Do you think you'll try camping again?"

"Maybe," I said. "Anyway, I'm definitely glad I came. It was kind of scary and frustrating sometimes, but there were plenty of fun parts, too."

That was true. There was a lot more to camping than I'd ever realized! Some of it was interesting or fun or cool, like campfire songs and learning more about nature and bug juice. Some of it wasn't so great, like latrines and falling in the lake.

But I was glad I'd tried all of it—and done my best to stay positive, at least most of the time. I vowed to remember that the next time something seemed new and difficult.

I was still thinking about that when Mom and Giggles picked me up later that day in the school parking lot.

"Hi, boy!" I cried as Giggles raced up to me, barking and wagging his short little tail. "I missed you, too!" I picked him up and hugged him.

"How was the trip, Amy?" Mom asked, hurrying over to help me with my bag. She looked worried.

I smiled. "Great," I told her. "Not perfect—but still great."

"Really?" She sounded relieved. "That's wonderful. We missed you at home, though. We didn't know what to do with ourselves without you!"

I dropped my bag by the car and gave her a hug. "I missed you guys, too," I said. "I'm really glad I went, though. Thanks for saying yes, Mom."

"You're welcome, Amy," she said, hugging me back. "I guess we need to realize you can handle more than we think. I'm proud of you."

I was proud of me, too. Because after this trip, I knew I could handle just about anything!

My Wilderness Overnight!

CAMP
FALLING LEAF

My trip was so much fun!

Me and the girls in our bunk.

Me and all the counselors.

Kim Wayans and Kevin Knotts are actors and writers (and wife and husband) who live in Los Angeles, California. Kevin was raised on a ranch in Oklahoma, and Kim grew up in the heart of New York City. They were inspired to write the Amy Hodgepodge series by their beautiful nieces and nephews—many of whom are mixed-race children—and by the fact that when you look around the world today, it's more of a hodgepodge than ever.